Mama Rex & T

Halloween Knight

by Rachel Vail

illustrations by Steve Björkman

SCHOLASTIC INC.

New York Toronto London Auckland Sydney
Mexico City New Delhi Hong Kong Buenos Aires

To Steve, who saw "a tribute to a tenderhearted child"
and breathes life and humor into every page of it.
—RV

For every child who dares to dream, and becomes a hero,
a princess, or even a tree, on Halloween.
—SB

ISBN 0-439-38471-0

10 9 8 7 6 5 4 3 2 1   02 03 04 05 06

Printed in the U.S.A.
First Scholastic printing, September 2002

Book design by Elizabeth Parisi

Contents

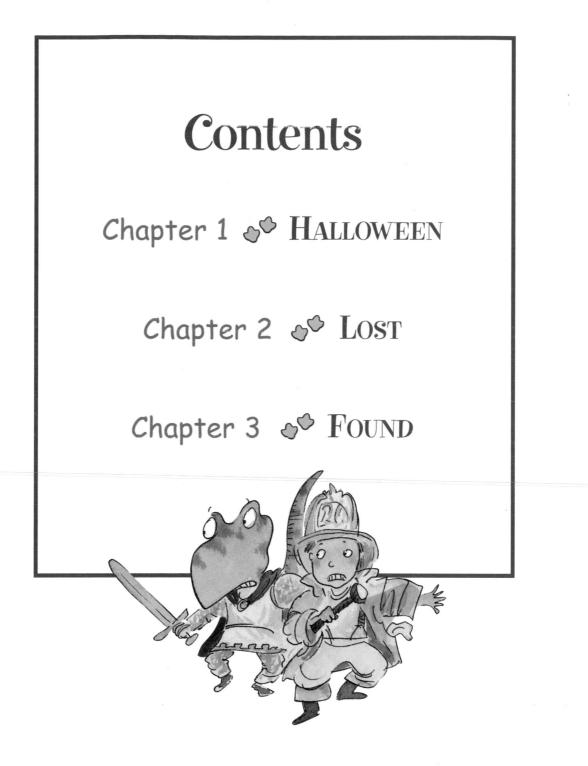

Chapter 1
HALLOWEEN

Mama Rex tried to grab T's hand. She got
whacked in the leg by a plastic pumpkin.

"Ah loob dip a dee-dee," said T.

"What?" asked Mama Rex.

"Ah fed, Ah loob dip a dee-dee," said T.

Mama Rex looked down at T.

A helmet covered his face, and made everything he said sound like nonsense with an echo.

"T?" asked Mama Rex. "I have no idea what you're saying."

T lifted the visor and grinned at Mama Rex. "I love trick-or-treating."

Mama Rex smiled. She loved Halloween, too.

T twirled around so his cape breezed up.

His sword smacked into a parking meter and fell on Mama Rex's shoes.

T bent over to pick up his sword, and his helmet fell off his head. A kid dressed as a bumblebee picked up the helmet and handed it to T.

"Thanks," said T, rubbing his head. "I like your costume."

"Thanks," said the bumblebee. She grabbed her father's hand to cross the street.

T smiled up at Mama Rex, but Mama Rex
wasn't there.
He spun around — and crashed into Mama Rex.

"There's a point in this helmet," said T.
"It sticks into my head."

He lifted the helmet to show Mama Rex.

"Oh, I hate that," said Mama Rex.

She juggled her things so she could hold both
the helmet and T's hand. "We have to stay
together," she said, as they crossed the street.
"I don't want you to get lost in the crowd."

As soon as they reached the curb, T let go and pretended to fence an invisible dragon.

"I'm a brave knight," said T. "I'm not scared."

Mama Rex took both T's hands and knelt in front of him. A pirate, a police chief, a prince, and a pair of tomatoes rushed by.

"Do you remember what to do?" asked Mama Rex. "If we get separated?"

"We won't," said T. "Let's go! Let's find Walter!"

"If we do, remember," said Mama Rex. "Go to the nearest tall thing, and stay there. I will find you."

"I know, I know!" said T. He turned around and yelled, "Walter!"

Walter was clomping toward T.
His firefighter helmet fell off.
Walter bent to grab it and dropped his
flashlight and goodie bag.
Then Walter's little sister, Gracie, bonked into
Walter and fell down on the sidewalk.

Mama Rex said hello to Walter's parents. T and Walter jumped around, dropping their stuff, and yelling, "Trick-or-treat! Trick-or-treat!"

Walter's mother said, "Gracie won't take off her sunglasses."

"She keeps bonking into everything!" said Walter. "It's great!"

"Gooo-ate!" said Gracie.

Walter's father handed T's helmet to Mama Rex.

"Thanks," said Mama Rex. "I was just telling T to stay..."

"Let's go!" yelled T.

"Trick-or-treat!" yelled Walter.

"Tickatee!" yelled Gracie, and bonked into a mailbox.

Chapter 2
LOST

T and Walter clomped ahead to the first building and waited in line.

When they got to the front, Walter held out his bag. T held out his pumpkin.

"Trick-or-treat!" they yelled.

A clown gave them each a candy.

Walter's went *shlip.*

T's went *thunk.*

T smiled.

That *thunk* was his favorite sound in the world.

Walter's father had Gracie in his arms. He pushed her goodie bag toward the clown.

Gracie buried her face in her father's shoulder and whispered, "Tickatee." The clown didn't hear, but he gave Gracie a candy, anyway.

Walter and T were on their way to the next door. There was no line at that one.

They walked right up.

A teddy bear gave them each a mint.

T and Walter said, "Thank you."

They didn't make faces at each other until after they walked away.

Behind them, Walter's mother and Mama Rex were talking about candy.

"So much candy!" said Mama Rex.

"Too much!" groaned Walter's mother. "Hey, slow down, guys!"

"I'm a carnivore," said Mama Rex. "But chocolate is my weakness."

"Me, too," said Walter's mother. "Luckily, my kids will devour it all tonight!"

T smiled over his shoulder at Mama Rex, who winked. T liked to sort through his candy every night in November and choose one piece for himself and one piece for Mama Rex.

T looked up at the fat, round moon.

On ordinary nights, when it was this dark, T was in his pajamas already.

"A knight at night," said T happily, brandishing his sword.

Walter stopped. "The Spooky One!" he whispered.

They were standing in front of a brownstone that had a smoky cauldron in front and eerie music playing.

T and Walter smiled nervously at each other.

Last year they had been too afraid to trick-or-treat at The Spooky One. This year they were on the borderline of old enough.

They inched closer and closer, crunching on the
fallen leaves.

T closed his eyes.

Walter opened his mouth.

They descended the stairs, pressed tightly together.

The entryway was dark and steamy.

Walter held his bag out.

T lifted his sword, then switched and held out
his pumpkin.

When they heard the *shlip* and the *thunk*, they
turned and ran up the steps.

"I wasn't scared," gasped T.

"Me neither," gulped Walter.

They stood blinking at each other for a few seconds, until they felt better.

"Next!" said T, trying to sound confident.

"This way?" asked Walter.

T looked where Walter was pointing.

Then he looked in the other direction.

He couldn't remember which way they'd come from. Or which way they'd been going.

"Where are the parents?" asked T.

Walter shrugged.

T said, "Maybe they're at the white building over there."

"Yeah!" said Walter.

Walter and T clomped up the steps of the white building.

A king and queen were singing while a jester played the keyboard. The queen gave T and Walter each three candies.

They looked like good ones, but T and Walter knew not to taste anything.

"Maybe they're outside," suggested Walter.

"Yeah," said T, and he followed Walter down the steps.

There were bunnies, bears, sheriffs, princesses, and plenty of parents.

Just not the *right* parents.

Meanwhile, Mama Rex had been chatting with Walter's mother. Mama Rex glanced down, saw a small dinosaur, grabbed its hand, and kept walking.

The small dinosaur asked, "Where's Polly?"

The voice was not T's voice, and Mama Rex didn't even know a Polly.

Mama Rex knelt down in front of the dinosaur and lifted her mask. Underneath was a little girl with red hair and blue eyes.

Mama Rex and the little girl were very surprised to see each other.

"Tickatee!" shouted Gracie, and ran away.
Walter's father chased her.

"Where are the boys?" Walter's mother asked
Mama Rex.

A man with red hair and blue eyes ran to
Mama Rex and the little girl.

"Hi, sweetheart," the man said softly to the
girl in the dinosaur costume. He lifted her in his
arms and said, "Thank you," to Mama Rex.

"That's OK," said Mama Rex. "I'm looking for
my own little dinosaur."

The moms climbed the steps of the nearest
building and looked inside, just as T and Walter
walked past the doorway, looking the other way.

"I'm not scared," whispered Walter.

"Me neither," whispered T.

Chapter 3
FOUND

Walter and T got out of the way of some laughing, big-kid wizards.

The moms got squeezed in the other direction.

"This is fun," said Walter, sadly.

"Hey," yelled T. "Mama Rex always says if we get separated, I should go to the nearest tall thing and stay there, and she will find me. And she'll find you, too, of course, in this case. Because you'll be with me."

"Yeah," said Walter. "Of course."

T and Walter looked for something tall.

"The buildings are all tall," said Walter.

"I think she doesn't include buildings," said T. "Hmmm."

T pointed at a very tall gentleman wearing a top hat.

Walter nodded.

Walter and T tried to follow him, but he was walking too fast.

"Maybe she doesn't include people, either," whispered Walter.

"Probably not," agreed T. "Lampposts?"

Walter nodded.

T and Walter ran to the nearest lamppost, leaned against it, and waited.

Meanwhile, Walter's father had caught Gracie and found the moms.

"Where are Walter and T ?" he asked, as Gracie restyled his hair.

Mama Rex was looking above their heads. "Near something tall, I bet."

Just then, the very tall gentleman wearing a top hat strolled by. Mama Rex checked behind him.

No T or Walter.

"Tall?" asked Walter's mother. "Why would they be near something tall?"

"To make it easy for us to find them," said Mama Rex, looking higher.

She saw the moon, the buildings, and the lampposts.

"Let's check lampposts," Mama Rex suggested.

Walter's father put down Gracie and said, "Gracie, please hold my hand. Gracie. Gracie!"

But Gracie was already off and running.

The three grown-ups chased her.
"She can't see anything!" yelled Walter's
mother. "Gracie! Stop! Oh, no!"

Gracie bonked into a lamppost and fell down on her bottom.

Her sunglasses fell off.

She blinked and said, "Hi, Wawa. Hi, T."

T looked down at the toddler beside his foot. "Hi, Gracie," he said.

"Gracie!" yelled Walter.

T and Walter raised their heads and saw their parents racing toward them.

Mama Rex lifted T and hugged him.

Walter's parents hugged both their kids.

"You did the right thing," whispered Mama Rex.

T smiled. "I wasn't scared," he said. "I knew you'd find me."

"Can we keep trick-or-treating?" asked Walter.

The parents looked at one another out of the corners of their eyes.

Some eyebrows lifted and some shoulders shrugged.

"OK," said Mama Rex.

"I guess so," said Walter's mother.

"If we must," sighed Walter's father.

"Hooray!" shouted Walter and T.

"Tickatee!" shouted Gracie.

T grabbed Mama Rex's hand as they strolled with their friends down the center of the crowded street, through the dark and sparkling Halloween night.